"Show and Tell"

Wendy K. Perriman

(and friends)

1995 - 1996

(Photograph by Expressly Portraits)

Best wishes Ed,
Wendy
Oct. 1997

Published by Inka Publications
P.O. Box 53, Madison, NJ 07940

ISBN 1-57502-426-8

Earlier versions of these poems appeared in:
"Feelings," Anderie Poetry Press (*Memorials*)
"Illya's Honey," Quarterly Journal of Poetry (*Invaders*)
"Womankind," Anderie Poetry Press (*When-*)
"Words of Wonder," Anderie Poetry Press (*Turning Point*)

Wendy K. Perriman is a member of *'The International Woman's Writing Guild,' 'Poetry Society of America,' 'The Academy of American Poets'* and *'Women Who Write'* (New Jersey).

Special thanks to the Madison Branch of '*Women Who Write*,' whose critiquing was invaluable!

Printed in the USA by

Morris Publishing
3212 E. Hwy 30
Kearney, NE 68847
800-650-7888

Formalist

I dislike the slackness of free verse;
hurling vocabulary
blind on a blank square
with bold pulsing passion and verve,
is as a novice aviator
stepping blithely from
a shiny aircraft
ten thousand feet high,
willing pale parachute
to spring forth,
tilt him on target.

And who is to say if he hits?

TABLE OF CONTENTS

INKA PUBLICATIONS POETRY SHOWCASE COMPETITION, 1996

SHOW AND TELL

_1995 - 1996_

To Grace, Jackie and Roberta

thanks for always being there

When -

In response to Rudyard Kipling's "IF-"

When you discover rules, which temper your life
Can often be remolded with a smile;
When options, split between career and housewife
May coexist together in a while;
When you can dress attractive on the outside
And on the inside still compete with Man;
When parents show your photographs with deep pride
Still strive to be the very best you can;

When lust has turned to love and there are choices
Where someone has to make a sacrifice;
When peace of mind is burned by multi voices
But in the end you know this is your life;
When children bring the joy and hate of bearing
And make demands you sometimes cannot meet,
Or turn from your advice and scorn your caring
And run away on strong rebellious feet;

When you can master skills enforced by others
And learn to cook and clean and iron and sew;
When you conform, and act as becomes Mothers
To starve yourself, allowing them to grow;
When you can pay the bills and balance check books
And still provide some fun along the way,
When even after birth, retain your young looks
To enjoy all the games he wants to play;

When you can maintain family and career
And be respected for your depth of soul;
When even under pressure you are still near
To bind the broken wing and to console;
When you can face the future of the black pit

And be enthusiastic for the new -
Yours is the World and everything that's in it
And - which is more - you'll be a Woman, too!

Cuckold

He did not feel the blazing comet trail
Of burning glances hurled across the fold
Between forbidden loves, the scorching Braille
Of hidden hands and promises untold;
The clues of muted voices, downcast eyes,
The purring of an empty telephone,
The hungry nights left vacant by surprise
With blackness, in the homeliness alone;
Without glimpsing the light, he never found
A wanting in his world, for space had rent
Past lives apart that once roved common ground
Replacing trust with voids of discontent.
What others know, will flare past pride to rage;
Her love sparks with a new star, half his age.

Rules Of Engagement

Clichés for a Successful Marriage

1.
To *know yourself* is imperative
in any contesting engagement,
love is a battle, life is a war
but prior thought can prevent estrangement.
Whilst no one is perfect, there are souls
whose flaws need a little assistance,
to strip to the bone old prejudice
overcoming stubborn resistance.
Try to change what you can never love
and to love what you will never change,
to give with feeling, without reward
to reward what you can rearrange.

2.
To *know your true aim* is important
and to have a fixed scheme to follow,
drifting doubt-driven relationships
go nowhere, for inside yawns hollow.
All planning should lead to happiness
the objective needs be consistent,
each phase builds on all previous ones
showing effort to be persistent.
Live presently for the future dream
but remember that future starts now,
a wedding is not a final deed
but a first step in sealing the vow.

3.
Know your enemy, Sun-tzu advised
understand where adversity waits,
a feline friend may signal an end
with such seemingly innocent dates.

Those who are jealous will compromise
will seduce and tempt for disaster,
they deem to destroy the perfection
seek to shatter the alabaster.
Beauty is often more vivid when
beheld as the prize of another,
the forbidden sin is beckoning
to chisel the lust from a lover.

4.
Always *know the situation* so
the initiative can be retained,
understanding various options
some aggression can then be retamed.
Surprise is a powerful weapon
harmful, harnessed to have an effect,
it may keep fear at bay, is useful
to compensate, interest and protect.
And results can sometimes be mastered
with strategy, used time and again,
which does not attack at the body
but successfully fights for the brain.

5.
Know to work as part of a team and
do not perform in isolation,
and never forget the importance
of effective communication.
When all eyes look to a single sun
the same light enhances each player,
and empowered by togetherness
both become a brave dragon-slayer.
Two islands cannot function without
a support network binding the parts,
and dual minds cannot find unity
until mutual trust seals their hearts.

6.
Know the value of simplicity
and the strength of a flexible plan,
but yet do not underestimate
the intelligence of fellow man.
There should be a fall back position
an emotional safe place to flee,
providing for each trapped, proud warrior
chance to salvage some lost dignity.
And it often pays to be wary
not to respond as fashions dictate -
there are many wasps trapped by sugar
which they realize, only too late.

7.
Know the best method of self-defense
is initiate the first advance,
thus commanding the situation
for there may only be that one chance.
Always dominate on the high ground
holding back something strong in reserve,
and never show when you are wounded
but instead beat back at their main nerve.
If you strike first, hit hard and heavy
be successful in the prime attack,
intentions can sometimes be thwarted
and what goes around, often comes back.

8.
Know just where to find hidden weak points
and remember to cover the flank,
your radar should spot the back-biters
so their black schemes will draw a white blank.
A true friend will never betray, but
an acquaintance or neighbor might try,
the warnings may be carefully coded
so a treason can softly slip by.

So hold up blind faith for good judgment
thinking with the heart and with the head,
trust takes may summers to blossom
but a single frost can kill it, dead.

9.
Know to reinforce your successes
is a maxim the Russians adhere,
life is a journey of challenges
and of memories that both will hold dear.
Yet in nature there are the wounded
so suffering must be expected,
but the hardships will be overcome
as the targets are redirected.
Strength is derived from adversity
which matures in the steps from childhood,
and character grows with our knowledge
so experience is always good.

10.
Know to choose the right ground for fighting
as Wellington said to his army,
for when *lions are led by donkeys*
their orders are usually barmy.
And many a battle is won by
having both feet on firm solid soil,
and many a marriage is ruined
when old arguments niggle and spoil.
To live for a lifetime in union
is quite possible, when you learn how
to be tolerant of each other
and never go to sleep on a row.

11.
Know that one must be realistic
expectations can sometimes be high,
that there will always be casualties

but the important thing is to try.
Know the consequence of ambition
and the cost to the home of career,
learn to balance your needs with others
when the demons of discontent near.
If love lies exhausted and withered
it is all right to halt and to pause,
some never commit further ground troops
when they think they have chased a lost cause.

12.
Know how to recognize achievement
there are small gains to reap every day,
alternative methods to fighting
when new compromise comes into play.
Some are never sure of victory
it can only be measured in years,
but learn nothing bad lasts forever
collectivity silences fears.
If you face life's hurdles united
and you reach a point bleeding and sore,
do not surrender - true love can still
lose a battle, and yet win the war!

Of All

Of all new hearts that entered a shared place
with legs entwined, in union of the soul
and glued together broken parts of whole;
of all the hearts there are, best has your face.

Of all smooth lips whose kisses left a trace
across scarred skin where time has chalked its toll
and aged, to rob the future of a goal;
of all the lips, yours freshen and embrace.

Of all sharp minds that seek familiar ground
and quest a sacred light, some common sound
and found contentment in a child most blessed;
of all the minds there are, yours is unbound.

In years ahead, temptation will be drowned;
of all fresh loves to come, you are the rest.

For Steven

I love you for all the insights you sigh
for times when you
tuck your tongue tight,
curbing control
permitting me
to etch errant errors, unchained.
I love you for questions you emanate
for answers you
fail to provide,
making me mold
with my own mind
the future as part of a whole.
I love you for haplessly holding on
for the bravery
of letting go,
so soul can seek
self perfection
returning with freedom at will.

Fine Line

Whenever darkness slowly shuts its fist
Around me in the starkness of new night
Crushing past enchantment in a mind mist,
Somewhere inside there always blinks your light;
Whenever hope snuffs thin like dusty smoke,
Worn waxy tears drip scalding from life's flame,
Breezes tease with echoes of past words spoke,
Consoles and breathes your precious ghosted name;
Whenever scorching time burns a wet hole,
Melts the wick to puddles of molten rain,
Childhood dreams blow further out of control,
Yet never rob the memories that remain;
Coming shadowed futures I can handle -
Love illuminates me with its candle.

Whenever darkness screws up its thick fist
To suffocate with starkness of new night,
Screaming sores are rubbed inside a mind mist,
Sense blinded by an iridescent light;
Whenever hope curls around in snuffed smoke,
Worn waxy tears drip scalding from the flame,
Breezes freeze with echoes of past words spoke,
Skin shudders at the mention of a name;
Whenever scorching time burns wide wet holes,
Wicks wither molten puddles of hot rain,
Menace yawns to roar apart, and controls
Past memories of pleasure which remain;
In the weaving shadows futures dandle -
Hate illuminates me with its candle.

Negative

Someone spat a photograph
this morning in my mail box,
viciously anonymous.
A bland brown envelope split
its scalding snapshot secret
which was smoky, grained and blurred
from some hidden-hole camera,
vividly caught your loved face
screwing up in ecstasy
with an unknown girl in bed
whilst sealing a deal, and fate.
Eighteen years for ten minutes!
Victim basted in honey
trapped tight in tender tanned thighs
gullible, not innocent
nor a virgin to this doped
deception, this tequila
tinged temptation. I burn, pricked
by your slick scorpion sting,
want to run far, to find some
dark to hide, calm my heart in
pussing with hate, hot with hurt.
I dwell on our wasted trust
on the loss of face, of faith...
and past opportunities.

Wounded

I am your friend so you confide in me,
I try to answer with integrity,
I have to offer some harsh honesty
And help overcome this duplicity.

He was your friend but now we are unsure,
He contaminated what once was pure,
He took your pride, nailed it on a skewer
And wore deceit, which left you insecure.

She was your friend but then betrayed all trust,
She took your man within her frenzied lust,
She popped the present with a heaving thrust
And left the future pouring into dust.

I am your friend and so appreciate,
I know the nuances which aggravate,
I offer options we can contemplate
And give some strength whilst you recuperate.

Madness

Inside an outside face
past movies are reviewed,
framed with fine distortions,
smeared by silent voices,
crunched pop on crisp corn crumbs:
destroy, destroy, destroy.

Ballets underwater
in Technicolor hues
bobbed along swift soundtracks,
pitched upon the primed pulse,
black blobs dotted red drops:
enough, enough, enough.

Cramped, constrained by life vice,
twisted things beyond thought
cowered in the back row
hidden from mind monsters,
the beefed-up fate of fools:
beyond, beyond, beyond.

Spools turned ticker-tacker
faded former talent,
image incoherent,
snipped short, cut the sequence
rolled back yellowed old reels:
replay, replay, replay.

Blame

This is where prejudice can lead...

to Buchenwald
Bergen-Belsen.

Germany's children are starving.

The Holocaust stains our conscience as
a yellow blur in history.
This land of brown shirts,
of beasts stamping bloodied boots
on the bones of the wealthy and frail.

I am a German. Not yet a Nazi.
I turn aside from plain truth,
in nodding I blindly accept.
Yes, I guess why the sky rains soot,
why thousands arrive at the station
from trains that run only one way
into the camp, never out.
And the smell...the smell...the smell
of a generation lost forever
which clings to the air and our drying clothes,
which hangs over this town in a death shroud.

One people, one Reich, one leader.
One people, one Reich, one leader.

I have a family. I have children.
I close my eyes to the facts
so it will not happen to them.

This is where prejudice can lead...

to Treblinka
Auschwitz. Dachau.

Germany's children are starving.

Foul genocide is fast contagious.
See our civilization ebb
through the brittle cracks
of a madman's psychosis
to snuff out the doomed with tyranny.

I am a soldier. I follow orders.
I learn to hate these damned Jews,
to strip all humanity bare.
Yes, I am shocked by the ovens,
shaved bodies piled high in mud trenches,
the look in the children's faces
as they hunger, starve then die.
And the smell...the smell...the smell
of a nation squashed, festering in filth
as disease and decay eat up fouled flesh
and swamp all of the camp in a tar pit.

One people, one Reich, one leader.
One people, one Reich, one leader.

I have a family. I have children.
I close my heart to knowledge
so it will not happen to them.

Afterwards

What were the thoughts of the crew
after the flash when they knew
Hiroshima was gone?

As they watched the toadstool cloud
what fears did they voice out loud
in awe and excitement?

When the boys flew home again
could they quantify such pain
for promise of freedom?

As reports came did they know
what happened at Ground Zero
to all of those children?

Are they haunted in their dreams
by a thousand melting screams
through innocent blackness?

Since Enola Gay returned
what lessons has mankind learned
of peace or compassion?

Policewoman

switching into battle mode
cruising the metropolis
daunted frayed dividing line
between them and us

tired eyes have seen it all
hate and greed and ignorance
self struggling to breathe beyond
the garbage and pus

experience has hardened
deadened all emphatic nerves
an automaton programmed
dealing without fuss

vision tarnished by past sights
myopic in Man's madness
striving towards amnesia...
no thoughts to discuss

Drops

When we are manacled, missing mercy
God sheers our shackles in the name of love
and redeems us all with communal drops
of hope-kissed blood and the bright bread of life.
Dusted down, smooth soothed, He returns free will
in a benevolence as limitless

as hearts in Heaven. There are limitless
chances to serve or stray but His mercy
is permanent and pure, for if we will
conquer offending thoughts, God will grant love
and forgiveness again and again. Life
is a jumbled journey of choices. Drops

of sin sear our spirits shut and the drops
weigh lead in the essence of limitless
eternity, leeching the after-life.
In the end we all cower for mercy.
If we believe in the power of love
we can rise above the transient will

and seek that state of grace, so that we will
enter Paradise, where the black deed drops
and crackles on the cinders of His love
before falling away to limitless
oblivion. But we must learn mercy
too and should offer it for others. Life

is a test: this is only the first life.
Man will always wish with wanting and will
not pause plucking pleasure without mercy,
will fail in the flesh as fulfillment drops
back to craving. His lust is limitless,
seeking salvation in secondary love

when only one sort satisfies - God's love.
Gaudy gratification in this life
poisons our purity with limitless
filth, and forces us further from His will
towards an abyss of evil which drops
in the fierce flames of Satan's slick mercy.

Clemency is love. When we fall He will
catch us and grant new life for *we are drops*
*in that limitless ocean of mercy.**

* *(Gandhi)*

Turning Point

I have trudged The Valley
fought seen shadows of death,
Slept through the reveille
felt flame tinged Devil's breath,
Suffered from a childhood
split wide by poverty,
Turned away from things good
took opportunity,
Said loose things of regret
done deeds I should have not,
Made loving hearts forget
then thought such sins would blot,
Spent years on other sides
under magical lures,
Cheap tricks to flex my pride
but lacking in real cures,
Then God gave out a gift -
cured core was finally won;
I felt my essence lift
the day I met my son.

Balloons

With the dawn of packed lives
sun yawns perfect circles
before setting us loose
at mercy of blind winds.

At birth we climb glibly
into life's gondola
wear the flat envelope
two sinners unrolled there.

In youth we sway freely
tug firm upon load lines
spin wild all directions
form frail quests to control.

Then eighteen breaks, rising
as crown strings are severed
can no longer pin us
to adult stale ground-dust.

For a brief time we soar
with ambition rustling
daring Godness, before
rushing soil sucks us down.

Weaning

I have shed
my past life
like a split
skin, wriggled
out of the
encasement,
left behind
innocence
which squashed me
sexless for
too many
shrunk summers.

Now you come
reminding
to stab as
sharpened barbs
past memories
deep within.
I grind them
down to dust
afraid of
old powers
in case they
cull me back.

Relative Thoughts

Where were you, old woman -
with your tight lips grimaced together
on the end of this telephone -
Where were you then, when it counted?

Your tape-worm tongue thrashes -
pokes puddles in bloody pockets of
forgotten childhood existence -
Your tape-worm tongue, full of malice.

So now you are lonely -
but I have no cracked caving conscience
where you are concerned, dear lady -
So now you are lonely and cross.

Your gnarly hands fidget -
tie knots in the hapless intestines
of those who adhere to your hiss -
Your gnarly hands could once have soothed.

I will not play martyr -
allow you to use up my goodness
plucking apart these close segments -
I will not play the games you lead.

I do not respect you -
can only recall your impatience
with past circumstances and youth -
I do not respect you in age.

You used up the family -
expected that special tight treatment
you never once earned through caring -
You used up the love of others.

I steel from your whining -
seeing pale through the selfish motive
and all the manipulations -
I steel from your wheedling voice.

You have nothing to give -
with feelings cold, shriveled and moldy
all chances now frozen beyond -
You have nothing to give I want.

Old Age Is Selfish

At the end, there is only left oneness.
The cage starts to creak
for lubrication,
asks technology
for some salvation,
self-absorbed, waiting
for decimation.
Old age is selfish.

Still, that last precious breath must be savored.
Poking the conscience
for blind attention,
desperately seeking
for intervention,
bribing the spirits
for some extension.
Old age is selfish.

There is only sole consideration.
Worries of burden
on caretakers wane,
all thoughts are reserved
for integral pain,
quality life dulled
for those who remain.
Old age is selfish.

Intruder

It's so nice to see you old friend
(yet I see we are overheard)
Time has passed, but we meet at last
(when did you son become that nerd?)
I've so many things to tell you
(but I thought you would come alone!
So hard talking with his gawking
and he's always curt on your phone.)
Did you hear the latest gossip?
(I'll try informing you in code!)
Strange eyes swelling at my telling,
he squats there, like a poisoned toad.

I include him in our discourse
tuning in to testosterone,
he grunts replies through bored ringed eyes -
we both wish you'd left him at home.
As you talk of your ex-husband
selecting carefully clipped phrases,
from greasy hair a reptile stare,
remotest of teenage phases.
When we order from the menu
he becomes enthusiastic.
(What can he glut inside that gut?
The answer is quite fantastic!)

He smirks as he orders seconds
(enjoying that I am paying)
When he can't eat that extra meat
I realize he's just playing.
So I'm calm, benign, forgiving
(I add up his waste in my head)
He farts out loud, uproots the crowd
as he stretches out, overfed.

I hurriedly end this meeting
no wiser once we're departed.
One jealous boy kills all our joy...
just like when friendship first started.

Promotion

Money should have
liberated

but instead it
subjugated.

These complex games
you scheme and play

have flushed all once
free-choice away.

Their gilded trap
snapped tight and caught

a name full owned
a future bought.

You have to run
to keep their pace

as gold now shows
its baser face.

It serves no help
to sigh or shout,

release will come
when use burns out.

When heat turns hot
with pressure set

thoughts slam down hard
cause raw regret.

Adrenaline
keeps you alive -

let's hope some peace
can still survive.

Flying

I thought that at last
we had landed in
butter, that these pressed
curled wings could shake off
grime, enjoy all the
opulence plastered
and spread before us.
But I was so wrong.
Even as we gaze
around covenants
of richness, all I
can feel is the bone
frost-bite of steel as
I level on life's
knife edge, and wait for
my skin to be snicked.

Argument

you are so alike
so vitriolic
wild words impassioned
full of rhetoric
when you disagree
wooden head to head
thick pride walls out all
the other one said
so you state your case
in a louder tone
as arrogant thoughts
fall on ears of stone
then both eyes narrow
while anger rises
you spit out venom
stinging surprises
then fine breeding slips
and the naked self
is exposed on view
stripped of all its wealth
vocabulary fades
replaced by swearing
ugly personas
kill without caring
then the dust dies down
you are split apart

but those forced to watch
wear the weeping heart

Two Weeks?

Spirits press closer
Hankering. Huddling.

Waiting the moment
Rebirth. Renewal.

Personality
Formatting. Forging.

Blueprint foundations
Ghost-shadowy ghoul.

Cells crackle, crinkle
Doubling. Dividing.

Each part pre-programmed
Vulnerable. Viable.

Life slowly unfurls
Archaic. Anchored.

In firm fleshy folds
Placenta pliable.

Sickening hormones
Control. Creating.

Stomach pumps rounded
Bloated. Balloon blown.

Breasts full and plumper
Tingling. Tender.

Love in the darkness
Uncertain. Unknown.

Miscarriage

Clots cloud the future
death drags down driplets
cramps create panic
all feelings freeze numb.

Hope hangs suspended
tear-tinged in trauma
options obliterate
as blood-baths descend.

Hospital

drip drip click drip drip drip
gray gurney trundles nightmares into day

pop pop slop pop pop pop
headboard touches marrow-sucked worm faced death

beep beep squeak beep beep beep
studwalls slice the diverse lives asunder

ring ring ping ring ring ring
curving creatures curl in fetal memory

drip drip click drip drip drip
snatches from an Outside cut through curtains

pop pop slop pop pop pop
whistling wretches suck for rasped revival

beep beep squeak beep beep beep
wearied hearts skip jigs along to flatline

ring ring ping ring ring ring
the lucky just leave dignity behind

Unbirthday

I have put downstairs the things I bought
from the racks of *Mothercare*,
and have packed away the tiny clothes
you will never get to wear,
and the Christening shawl lies crisp and white
as empty as its own lace,
and in this New Baby's First Year Book
there will not be found your face,
and the plastic toys your brother gave
lie hidden inside a box,
and a pink hairbrush lies unemployed
without stroking your blonde locks
and the Eeyore doll is lonely for
he has no warm knee to kiss,
and the nights stretch full of emptiness
from a memory amiss,
and these little shoes will never feel
the soles of your curled-up feet,
and puzzles will all remain unsolved
with the jigsaw incomplete,
and Piglet will not get to dance on
the borders around your wall,

for you were just too fleeting a love
to be ever born at all.

Willow

wisened wild crone wends
towards whispering waters
sips secrets inside

Late Snow

The myopic sun squints like a
pale cataract
through an egg-white
foggy eye
blinking sleepy fat flakes
like wan scabs
on a lukewarm
bitter earth.

Shapeless lumps form in the gloaming
to ball away
identity
as the grass
is devoured by foam,
and fresh shoots
snap in broken
infancy.

Coldness chills courtship in squirrels
scuttering from
lust to hunger
again, much
confused by returning
to ice land,
when sticky buds
boil and plump.

Spring Sonnet

Smudged sun bids blighted whiteness drip away
and creaks its eyeball round from frosty blue,
bent snowdrops yawn, unfurl clocked heads to May
through spongy cogs, impregnated with dew.
Impatient taut trees itch to spark and bud,
with bolts of bursting fissure lean limbs groan,
a crocus heaves and splatters through the mud
where blizzards shed their scaly layers of bone.
Clockwork squirrels peck and tick through snarled bush
drenched with decaying debris spawned from yard,
feathered trilling pierces the beige hush,
unoiled responses screech, their lyrics jarred.

When nature winds the winter watchman in
the symphony of springtime can begin.

Discovery

Just like Columbus
touching virgin sand
I wade through waters,
mounds of pitching gold,
leaving impressions
in untamed beauty.
Unknown cove is ringed
with creamy cloudbursts
whipped far out to sea.
A thin fringe of palms
conceals the entrance
to this perfection.
Multitudinous
butterflies dip, dive
on heat-baked currents,
with buttercup wings
flapping me away.
Fast frothing waves groan,
We are discovered!
then force me to shore.
The sun fades ashen
bathed in shadows; and
warns of Man to come.

Bleed Out

Emerging viruses crash forth
along the Kinshasa Highway.

Lush-leaf leapers are left behind
as hot agents hunt the new cells
for biological burnout.

Marburg and Ebola burst, as
fresh twenty-first century plagues.
HIV already well-spread
in far, fatal infiltrations.

These armies are hypermutant
with no cures and scant prevention,
for four billion years have festered
in caves and flesh of Africa,
hidden hot-housed in fierce forests
species jumping, slick and rampant.

But the human race amplified
bringing threats of termination
to the biosphere, which fights back
with its own messengers of death
in defense against destruction.

Man has become a parasite
sucking the life blood from its host.
The Earth's immune system bites back
pruning this threat, to extinction...

as the pulse of nature throbs on.

Desert

The wilderness embraces in its sigh
Gilds golden life with radiant wind-spun dust,
Fresh generations roam in wanderlust,
New ages form. Millenniums pass by.
Saguaro cacti pierce an endless sky
While Prickly Pears arch down to brush the rust,
Jack Rabbits lop and skid with shy mistrust
As snakes release their rattling battle cry.
Sunrise turns to peach behind torn blue buttes
Harsh noon heat soon bakes smooth wood marble white,
Thick shadowed silence follows eagle's flight
Snapped broken by faint crunch of cowhide boots.
This untamed land continues out of sight;
Within its depths brave futures pave their roots.

Night Music

a half-strangled
cockerel
crows the dark bark

tom cat prowl howls
on the lone shore

bug staccatos
gunning far stars

rain jigging on
calm palm
clapping the mud

Invaders

One hot afternoon in May, the garden was tied with strings
from a hundred abseiling caterpillars, on a day
surreal and nerve-nipped, as their military coup crowned
them kings.
One hot afternoon in May.

The cobwebs spun over their territory kept Man at bay
yet they had conquered all without weapons, sharp claws
or stings.
Camouflaged in black, warriors glistened in the door way

dangling on threads, with the power an invasion force brings.
From the tree tops they glided and deep in the grass they lay
waiting for nature to elevate on gossamer wings.
One hot afternoon in May.

Feeding Time

shrimp colored jelly bean
shivers
caged cornsnake sniffing meat
quivers
sightless exposed mouse frets
sucking
split tongue licks stilled silence
bucking
hours in blackened fright
waiting
slides towards preordained
fating
prickled skin registers
moistness
lost to new blackened womb
voiceless

Alligator

Silent submersible
ancient and ageless
you stare through patient eyes
in tree-felled stillness
waiting...

Able amphibian
dormant and deadly
you jeer through zippered jaw
in ghastly greeting
watching...

Recalcitrant reptile
blistered and battered
you soak your steaming skin
in sullied shallows
hiding...

Perfect prone predator
adroit and agile
you sniff through half-sunk snout
the slack and sickly
plotting...

White Tiger

The beauty queen struts,
forms a sultry pose,
dazzling sky eyes flash
above classic nose.
Well-groomed and tranquil,
each blonde hair in place,
confident aura
surrounds streamlined face.
Glazed by the spotlight,
her minions admire
sensual motions
sprung tight with desire.
She sweeps the catwalk
changes direction,
shapely legs pivot
no imperfection.
She stretches her neck
cruises down the aisle,
displays frosty teeth
the glint of a smile.

She can tell from my gaze
I declare her the winner;
I can tell from her stare
she would have me to dinner!

Hawk

From sullen skies falls a silent fire-flash
Of forged copper feathers beneath bronzed cloak.
Pantalooned talons mechanically poke
Crisp termination of freedom's last dash.
Stony eyes challenge as clashing claws lash
And brutal beak binds in a strangled choke,
White bib blood-basted as specks start to soak
Leaving splatters gored from the grizzled gash.
Victim knows nothing as brown night descends
Darkening daylight with chilled instant fear,
Just a stir in the air and then paining,
As the outwitted squirrel comprehends
That a violent swift ending closes near,
In completion of nature's cruel training.

Battle Cat

self-centered scavenger
scrawny and scab-crusted
skeleton survivor
on slim spindled legs

with skin stretched and rib taut
quick-witted and quirky
stubble-maned and sore-specked
on ribbon string frame

gray-grizzled and grubby
gaunt, grimy and grungy
fur greasy and flea-flecked
a pause on pained paws

weary and wound-weeping
wary, of fickle face
rickets-wracked and mangy
a matted mauled mog

Whale:

free flowing shadow
forms a mottled coal rock bridge
spits fountains of spray

Seal:

soaking up chilled sun
small face squirms in ecstasy
at peace with the world

Dolphin:

wave dancing spirit
curves, arching and spiraling
in marshmallow froth

Shark:

grim soldered phantom
metallic and menacing
top link in the chain

Big Brother

Water refracts as a neon green quilt,
Gilds marble sleek skin in electric frost.
The dolphins roll by with a flick and lilt
Of silver muscle, no playfulness lost
To maturity or time, in their own
Realm unchanged. Blueberry ripples adorn
Pale bellies, gleaming glints of opal stone.
They smile at the raw future, as if born
Innocent creatures, as yet unafraid
Of cold progress and new technology.
Fins cut to surface and there are displayed
Fine aerial acrobats of the sea,
Who screech and caper, court Man as a friend...
Maybe aware of the depths they depend.

Skunk

She rolls to my back porch to die,
a bristle of fur starved by snow
forbidding entry to her lair.
Fringe falls limp over ember-red
eyes, trapped in a huddle of frost.
Frayed tail drags behind her like rope,
snout nose still sniffing and rooting
for food that cannot save. She folds
fast shut. Waits to expire. Her tired
face dripping, as its once-white streak
of glamour, fades slowly into
an acceptance of gray.

Hamster

Hamster,

I think you were made
when God recycled the leftovers
from Creation.
A bear's
blueprint contracted
to a honey warm cub, was rolled in
brown Coney fur.
There were
not enough tails left
instead you were tapered to point like
a burly bee.
Feline
ears suggest battle
scalloped but tatty, and speckled with
horse-dappled smears.
Sleepy
face from the dormouse
is delicately docile, fresh with
a gerbil nose.
You were
spiked with long rat-teeth
pricked with whiskers from the seal that you
imaged at birth.
Squirrel
blood leaps in your veins
propelling the wingless acrobat
on gecko toes.
Sinking
sun send you scuttling
to yawn and stretch out your ferret frame
almost boneless.
You can

mine maps like the mole
then slink through the hungry night snuffling,
seeking a world
without corners.

Nanook

At the edge of our world frigid seas heave
and moody bruised clouds crack scuffed sky,
tramping through tundra the great white bears weave
ungainly on coy pigeon-toes.
Languidity ripples in furrowed manes,
lines camouflaged inside glass rocks,
smelling the silence smart predatory brains
detect seal and gaming begins.
Breath hiss stifles a snort in thin coldness
a warning, before the attack.
Roaming undaunted, with concealed boldness
as raw wolves in soft sheep disguise.

The Solitary

The leopard prowls alone
half hidden and obscure;
balled muscle, firm as stone
sly-footed, swift and sure.

Half hidden and obscure
on quivering plains of heat;
sly-footed, swift and sure
she drapes her lair with meat.

On quivering plains of heat
in shadows and torn shrubs;
she drapes her lair with meat
to feed three squabbling cubs.

In shadows and torn shrubs
the zebras drink close by;
to feed three squabbling cubs
another's young must die.

The zebras drink close by
her silent spring will kill;
another's young must die
so hers can eat their fill.

Her silent spring will kill
then in the trees she'll lie;
so hers can eat their fill
but soon they'll say good-bye...

Then in the trees she'll lie
balled muscle, firm as stone;
but soon they'll say good-bye...
the leopard prowls alone.

Horseback

hoof hops
trotting
clipping carpets
of squat flowers,
pricked with purples
laced with lemons
under tropical trees,
in tangled tunnels...
tripping towards the beach

bent bones
bouncing
shifting skeins of
silt-salted sand,
washed and wave worn
pale and puckered
punctured by pumice peaks,
gray-ground and glistening...
splitting the sea to surf

Bird Watcher

I spy you, camouflaged by twenty years
Hiding still in the usual habitat,
Slim among smoky reeds, wading in beers
Observing the posing sly pussycat.
You preen before me displaying cool tones
Give me the gaze that once lured me to bed,
No longer ensnared by your peacock bones
I banter through memories, hurts left unsaid.
Decades and daring give spit to my speech,
Still your feathers lie flat, quite unperturbed
But through stone-set mask those lost eyes beseech,
Makes old conscience flutter, vaguely disturbed.

Because you were rooted, I purred good bye -
Because of my claws, you still cannot fly.

Games Lesson

It's twenty three years
since I stood on this grass
in my brother's old socks
cast in crusty mud,
wearing cheap football cleats
with my new birthday stick
playing hockey, scything past clods.
I can see us all now -
wearing pleated blue skirts,
each crooked initial
embroidered by pain
in the needlework class,
and those serge navy pants
pinned to our vests for protection.
We'd scrabble for bibs
wanting not to be left
abandoned in goal mouth,
fought to grab glory
as cruel center-forward
who bullied off first,
and long before any whistle.
Games would seem endless
with cheers marked by bloodspots;
the threat of showers reigned.
We vicious bitches
were stripped in submission
to run the ruled gauntlet
of untempered water and tears.

I Never Had A Sister

only you
oldest, dearest
closest, farthest
friend.
Trust bloomed like our sprouting breasts
we played at
danger, anger
couture, pleasure
fast.
Almost incompatible
I recall
match stick, homesick
slapstick, lovesick
you.
New continents have shifted
way apart
untied, wet eyed
good-byed, Stateside
me.

Yet always left is
us.

Tracks

A poem to celebrate 700 years as a market town

Who knows when Chircheham rose from muddy tracks
and Saxons claimed this fertile soil their own?
Roman armies walled these hills, marched off, then
time ground garrisons back to brick-red dust
and darkness fell on history. But lives
continued to shepherd, weave, cut peat and

discover God. The church, built from faith and
wood between two streams, was nestled by tracks
of farmland, and rang over simple lives.
1296 brought a charter to own
a market. Fishstones were placed around dust,
a circle of strength, linking cycles. Then

came days when knights rode with the Red Rose. Then
battlements boasted bold victory and
helped create an Empire from the war dust.
Soon folks found fate forging tentative tracks
towards the phase when the world was its own.
But a *great sickness* struck, stole many lives

and The Pennines darkened with loss. Young lives
bled into Pendle Hill, bewildered. Then
black spite was checked, sense came into its own,
grasped new knowledge from the Grammar School and
minds shone through past ignorance. Some saw tracks
led outside so they brushed off the old dust

of prior generations. Others found dust
in the chimneys and mills, lost their thin lives
to poverty and workhouse. Some soil tracks
were hoof-honed, then criss-crossed by cartwheels, then
cobbled as travelers trekked towards inn and
ale. Soon the Gentry folk fattened, to own

factories that wove Kirkham ugly, their own
worlds fair. Clogs cropped into this era. Dust
blew through *The Pride of the Fylde*. Wars called and
the sovereign was offered our virile lives.
Moor Street took the one bomb unperturbed. Then
tough townsfolk cheered, as the tanks tunneled tracks

into the dust of dictatorship, then
those same tracks brought the boys back to their own.
From Doomsday, and to doomsday, Kirkham lives!

Myths And Legends

A poem to celebrate 700 years as a market town.

There's a rural town, name o' Kirkham
that's noted for clogs and for boots
and many a family that lives there
can trace back to Doomsday, its roots.

With Romans, we ain't much acquainted,
they left some pot bits in the earth
but longtime before that, some Saxons
had given this little place, birth.

We know nowt about the Dark Ages
except the red rose was ours,
when we thrashed them Yorkies to puddin'
outside of Lancaster's towers.

When t'Civil War broke out in Green Lane
Lord Derby beat Cromwell's blokes black.
For a time, soldiers raged and pillaged
but Kirkham ignored all attack.

About then, a Mrs. Houghton birthed
a monster-like baby they said.
She replied, that this was much better
than having to nurse a Roundhead!

There were witches once dunked in't duck pond,
You could have your wife dipped at will!
Stories of women stuffed in barrels
findin' death upon Pendle Hill.

Then, murder was really quite common,
Peg Hall's slit throat left bloody smears.
They say that her ghost walks The Crofts now
and in a white nightgown appears.

The kids know that Mowbreck Hall's haunted,
a catholic priest, it's been said.
Some tell of strange visions and fires seen
and no local went near, for dread.

The cotton mills covered their scandals
as old opened cellars revealed.
The young girls' disgraces were buried
in walled tombs their scared masters sealed.

So many pubs for a small town that
I'm surprised any work got done!
When they wanted to build the new church
first they had to get rid o' one.

And when motor cars came to Kirkham
a chap wi' a flag walked ahead.
So astonished was Mr. Boulton
he was killed by the first one, dead.

But there's always tattlin' in small towns,
who did what, where and when, with whom
and even though much is uncovered
some secrets still go to the tomb.

So what will folks tell about our lives
the things we get up to, today?
Good stories are turned into legends
and myths come from someone's hearsay.

Before Kirkham's glory is over
there'll be other stories to tell.
The future may gawp at *our* antics,
quote characters we now know well!

My England

I search for the lime fields of childhood,
sunshine trapped in the thin rods of corn,
the wind blowing tendrils of horse grass,
for hills climbing free into smooth skies;
but I find nature deconstructed,
decayed factories jawed in graying smog
with rust-weeping wounds spawned like cancers,
brown funnels wagging warnings of doom...

I visit fresh ponds of my memory,
frog-spawn packed sparkling in jam jars,
a lesson in brave evolution,
the brilliance of new life revealed;
but I recoil from repugnant waters,
see yellow crusts scummed like a chancroid,
choked dead under gangrene and garbage
with weeping weeds groping for ground space...

I wade along beaches past trodden,
scan sculptures of sand and excitement
whilst secretly toeing the treasures
for pink pearly jewels in the making;
but tacky tar seersucks my footsteps,
condoms crab in the seaweed and slush,
lost lugworms lie buried in plastic,
the jellied foam froths septic pustules...

I travel through routes of a past life
seeking the strong child with future's face,
for burning blue eyes wild with wisdom,
lips crinkling a warm line of welcome;
but I glance at the grimy daughter
staring warily through the gate bars
accepting all adults as danger,
unsafe even in her own garden...

My England.

On Birthing Thanatos - Dunblane, 1996

Forgive me little ones. I did not know
My legacy, spawned on a sterile ward
So many moons ago, would leave a thing
That damned bloody. A stunned world is now less
Your sweetness. Was evil there at the start?
When rooting, had it already begun

To suckle his small soul towards the gun?
A punishment past pain. Yet even now
He manipulates. Yes, this is his art -
His Picassos bent screaming and awkward
Meld into memory, melt motionless;
Your passing from beauty into something

Sacred and scarce, safe with God. A loathing
Assaults and shell-shocks, slivers of shotgun
Shards, that I mothered this monster, lawless
And sick. Am I to blame? I need to know,
As my cold conscience coils itself inward,
What sniffling slight, split and shattered apart

His whole. Perhaps there was always that part
Robed in darkness; that raw anger. Something
Perverse, which proudly propelled him forward
To doomsday, wedded to love of the gun.
Is he gratified, grafted to Hell now?
Our town is swamped by an Outside, helpless

To comfort. Your many parents, childless
And void of faith. So much red dust. A part
Of humanity rests in ruined snow,
Alongside redundant bright flowers, breathing

Prayers for innocence; the mourning begun.
Can the adults feel again, as they ward

His presence from nightmares, turning toward
Torn tomorrow, scarred shells suffering less?
As survivors, struck still by the gray gun,
Forage for fragments that once made a heart,
They ask, how could there be such a black thing,
This horror home-grown? You just never know.

Eyes peer outward to Oklahoma now,
Seek some thing, some fragment of hope to bless,
For a healing begun, and a new start.

Englishman

You did not want to meet me,
your countryman abroad,
an initial assessment
thought I should be ignored,
for you are such a big shot,
a personality
and I seem just a housewife,
a no one, unworthy.
You judged me by appearance,
a number not to dial,
my presence is a nuisance
I read your chilly smile,
but one day you may realize
you should have met my eye
and then you might have noticed
as talent passed you by.

Osmosis

many months dormant
spent in absorbing
this alien culture, America
rooting through vinyl
sipping in glamour
succumbing to sucking sugar and vice
until all is one
and the lily blooms

Return To Niagara

we glide down the spine of the USA
we glide down the spine move move
we glide down the spine move

the rhythm of night runs blackness to gray
the rhythm of night move move
the rhythm of night move

trees stand as sentinels
lining our path
twin rails are framing
the greasy slick track
Canada waits in the
simmering dawn
Niagara humming
to welcome us back

floating on pockets invisible air
floating on pockets move move
floating on pockets move

on through the daytime and fast towards night
on through the daytime move move
on through the daytime move

Thundering Water

Morning. Dragon's breath rises from steam pit,
west wind whispers wondrous secrets as it
cloaks the Falls in cloud. Spiraling gulls sweep
and shriek. Gilded showers silver forth froth
nibbling on edges of torn time-worn cliffs.
The gorge hugs its past, creeps back to nature.

Noon. Hot sunshine melting on molten jade
swirling, spilling in shining cascades while
Spirit of Sacrifice sleeps in his crag.
Gold sky reflects on shimmering marble
where crumbling rocks weep to waters below
sculpting stepping stones far into futures.

Afternoon. Bold Thunder God wakes and yawns
an echo down his canyon. Darkness cloaks
tight bright skies, mugs the air. Fat rain drips fill
a white chilled cauldron, bubbling up, boiling
as lace edged waves. Rising river belches
scum stained scars, aroused by firestung fury.

Evening. Pocked raging ripples pitch and pound
blackened but steely, cloaked in hidden mist
as sweeping stomach retches on strewn rocks
in a bog fog below. Spirit bellows
his moody melody down through the clouds
of generations...towards the rapids.

Navajo

and progress came
in white man's name...
reservation
relocation
confiscation...
negation

fought to belong
danced to pale song...
isolation
deprivation
degradation...
dictation

failed in attack
no turning back...
legislation
castigation
liquidation...
cessation

Memorials

Row upon row of white Georgia marble
Arlington Cemetery displays its pride,
Line upon line of star-spangled banners
Marking a memory to those who have died.
At the tomb of the unknowns, a hot sun
Beats time with the cyborgs changing their guard.
There is so much pomp, death held in glory,
An eternal flame. No sacrifice marred.

Slab upon slab forms the black wall elsewhere
As Vietnam Veterans honor their own,
Name upon name squashed huddled together
No flags, no flowers. Just medals on stone.
This war is not over for those who keep
Vigil in leathers and old combat gear,
They fight for friends still missing in action -
and I find there is more dignity, here.

Bypass

On a subway bench she sat
in a station off Times Square
a black lady in a hat
catching people unaware.

In a station off Times Square
she shouted to commuters
catching people unaware
they rushed to their computers.

She shouted to commuters
she had just had surgery
they rushed to their computers
so she gave a call to me.

She had just had surgery
she was told to then go home
so she gave a call to me
when she found herself alone.

She was told to then go home
her body old and broken
when she found herself alone
without a two-tone token.

Her body old and broken
a black lady in a hat
without a two-tone token
on a subway bench she sat.

Sniper

I am antisocial
aloft in my playhouse,
unnoticed and itchy,
eyeing toy targets
through my magic scope.

One will be sacrificed
nailed between thin black cross,
minute microbes who swarm
in my petri dish.
I am spoilt. Broody.
Focusing laser beam
scans warped weaving wavelengths
across steamy sidewalks.
An insect glows red
in the juicy light.

They all look the same now
packed corn, ripe for popping
who will crack on command.
This is too easy...
my finger grows bored.

Jackie

Cold bullets cut the thread
Swift spun sweet breath away,
A husband's life was shed.

Brown splatters blotched from red
Eyes widened in dismay,
Cold bullets cut the thread.

He groaned, grasped tight his head
Confusion split the day,
A husband's life was shed.

Another flash of lead
Tore glints of hope astray,
Cold bullets cut the thread.

Spent bouquet petals bled
She held sick fear at bay,
A husband's life was shed.

Taut heart sensed he was dead
Close in pale arms he lay,
Cold bullets cut the thread.
A nation's life was shed.

Tasting The Apple

THE FIRST SIN:
Vomit-colored bubbles scum the edges of The Hudson. The
swollen body floats like excreta in the harbor, is first
spotted by the 'Bladers as they skate at dusk, with a deadly
pallor of septic light forming in the dark. Volatile sin
forges an erasure of identity, and her pale breath is
extinct now, another Jane Doe, the outlet of pure anger

unchecked and unrepentant. The fetid calf transcends anger.
She bobs obscenely, like an aquatic glow-worm paying the
price of vulnerability and risk. Surfing The Edge at first
seemed exhilarating. The intoxication of deadly
adrenaline pulsed in her slick Wall Street dreams, but there is sin
in all desire and the palpable price I require now is

fear. You feel it, smell it, taste it. Soon you shall see what it is.
This bloated scapegoat personifies my Beast, reflects anger.
Someone has crossed past your boundaries and cruelly fouled up the
smog you all fought to share, debased it. This time is not my first!
Unknown body stripped of dignity, grins at this world, deadly
with glass-eyed knowledge. CNN News - come revel in this sin

and titillate your viewers. Show them my art and let them sin
as hungry minds absorb the gore. O what a pleasure it is
to parade my skills, demonstrate the purest form of anger
and be immortalized at last. No one ever noticed the
placid me. I have been much more interesting since the first.
Now my sudden, hidden vengeance coils, venom-white and deadly.

When she looked into this handsome face, which cakes over deadly
cracks with charm, did she ever detect there the simmering sin
tucked beneath the flawless pores? She told me that a stranger is
just the lover you do not know. But when aroused by anger
peeling mask reveals the core, the molten spew from within the
pit, which wants and in its craving, will destroy. There can be first

one chance: submit to and appease my lust. Yes, there can be first
a subjugation in sacrifice of Self, before deadly
thoughts blot black the brain. But then, with slight provocation, the sin
can ceremoniously surface, and the red of rage is
the overwhelming passion. In an orgasm of anger
there is release. My will is law. I am God and she is the

totem, the victim, the lamb. The breaking of trust will come first
then the breaking of nails, of neck, of life as immoral sin
elevates conscience, numbs my heart and quantifies this anger.

THE SECOND SIN:
Carnality switched tracks, as I tossed in the gray night and saw then
with cat-like globes, the clarity of that perspective which came
into focus, a recognition at the source of my greed.
No longer would *his* body suffice, with its rotting folds as
scaly as bark. Plastic-stuffed mouth could never pleasure me the
way it had in beginning. A third *his* age, I was second

wife and beneficiary. But had ever, for one second,
I loved the man? Or was my beauty ensnared by image, then
diamond-refracted promises? Insatiable desires came
alive in many formats, but pure passion pussed green with greed
and love became a lust of rage. To compensate for youth as
best *he* could, *he* pampered me and fueled the fever, buying the

woman *he* wanted. Avarice is a bottomless vice. The
chasm grew wider and hungry with time. Each fragile second
gnawed at my glamour. Each day the creaking gate moved and moaned. Then
cupidity crept from coolness to consciousness, and came
packed with plottings - the ultimate sin. Painted talons of greed
started tapping a Morse-code of death to an accomplice as

fallen as I, who wooed me with covetous eyes each day as
he trained me to run. Passion proved poison, as we poked in the
bed that *he* owned, in basest communion. A stolen second
of bliss in a wily web of words. Crystallized details then
emerged. Rapacious and ravenous rantings flowed, and they came
with a vengeance. He succumbed to my body, then to the greed.

Pained plans were finalized. In duplicity, we were a greed.
Wildly wanton with wine at the *old man's* expense, we watched as
the hour of *his* death approached. There was now no repeal and the
Grim Reaper grinned from the shadows whilst counting the souls. Second
thoughts were snuffed shut, green vapors blew them out. No mercy left. Then
came the climax, the killing, the call from the Police. Then came

the funeral cortege and the face hid by black veil. Then came
the money, that malignancy which struck *him* down dead; the greed
in the eyes of the relatives who preyed in their mourning, as
the will was revealed. Harsh words and accusations flared but the
family consoled this widow, not suspected for one second
being tear-stained and hurt from the loss. Wore black for one week then

I vanished, on the same day my trainer left town. Now glows greed
as he looks into my face, flushed with fervor as I just came,
but I smile at his back and scheme. He will not be my second.

THE THIRD SIN:
Transsexuality slashes my psyche, lust and envy
at war with testosterone for femininity follows
me, coveting the satin and fur. The yin and yang lie next
to libido, a mad moral battle for dominance in
a body confused and abased. Such a torment of mind this
creates, punishing the prisoner snapped shut in this sequence

of chromosomes, predetermined and permanent; this sequence
which forced me to yield for twenty-one years, whilst eying envy
watched the woman I wanted to be, flourish. It now follows
and plagues all waking and working. I painfully plan the next
phase of transformation, craving the catharsis present in
my heart. There is a penalty for yearning and mine is this:

ostracization, ridicule and violence, being in this
liberal society, the subject of a long sequence
of pain and rejection. Men are only allowed to envy
men; penis-proud, virile. A denial of feeling follows
the macho male, who struts and swaggers sublimely to the next
conquest, repressing urges frowned upon and forbidden in

our culture. Through fake eyelashes I view the phony world, in
women's shoes l seek to find a meaning to my life in this
scheme of being. The name was the first thing changed in the sequence.
Soon came clothing, a sensual spite, an orgy of envy
as I lavished my lust in lace. Depilation then follows,
pore-painful procedures which primp, prime and prepare for the next

phase, the silk-swathed seduction of sensitive skin. But the next
stage requires more commitment; chemical changes congeal in
my hormones, melting machismo, resetting the wrongs and this
will continue past surgery in the delicate sequence,
slicing and separating the folds of flesh, to end envy.
The butterfly emerges from the cocoon and it follows

fluttering in the frail winds of its fantasy. It follows
a dream, an apple that rots once bitten, and the tearful next
realization of a desolate illusion. Hidden in
this body is the image of the God I deny and this
is my penance. I will never erase His presence. Sequence
upon sequence will haunt my heritage and always envy

for the missing years. I try to imitate females, but next
to one, these womanly wiles lie clumsy and false. What follows
close in that shadow of sham, will smother me with its envy.

THE FOURTH SIN:
Treasons of terrorism tear up your tarmac. Another
explosion bites deep at the vain lives which preen in this home of
the brave, made divisible by dastardly devices. The
land of the free permits me to bomb your boastful buildings, set
fire to superior skyscrapers, daringly demonstrate
my contempt for all your arrogance and insolent fine pride.

You thought you were invincible! Well others also have pride
and honor equally demanding. It will take another
war to restore our dignity, but this battle will be of
a different format and you will yield to our rules. Go seal the
borders in hateful hegemony but the cells are pre-set,
already in place, as today's daring deed will demonstrate.

This irony of low order explosive will demonstrate
the parallel of our power to your people, who take pride
in star-spangled ideology thinking of another
time when they spilled foreign blood, meddling in the affairs of
distant lands: Iran, Iraq, Somalia, Lebanon...the
list goes on and on but when the bombs bite home you get upset.

That American psyches just cannot comprehend the set
patterns of fear London and Paris know, serves to demonstrate
your naiveté. You are not immune, cannot hide in pride,
for even if you catch me there will always be another.
Fertilizer and fuel oil forge a friendship in my blood of
vengeance and I will die for your damned destruction amidst the

carnage. Precision planned, my plot perfected, I wait in the
rented shell with the deadly detonators primed full and set.
My life ticks shut with the itchy button, but it demonstrate
my commitment to jihad; my sacrifice atones for pride.
Soon the violent volcano will spew forth fire, another
atrocity to rock your dust. I shall fade unaware of

my consequences. Coffins will line your streets, processions of
pomp, a writhing worm of piano keys whose notes will pierce the
silence, some large, some small, some black, some white, but all of them set
in a ceremony to respect and grieve; to demonstrate
further paradox, that many cannot afford such a pride -
their costs must be met by the conscience and funds of another.

I have earned my shiny place in paradise, a martyr. Pride
makes the mourners rebuild. A sin, but one which will demonstrate
a new day shall dawn for New York City. Always another.

THE FIFTH SIN:
Silenced by status he works; slave labor to cover our sloth
in the brain-blunting boring banality which for him is
redemption from homespun poverty. Opportunities here
wait, for the audacious. An illegal alien and on
the run from authority but muscled, held muzzled by the
law. He will tackle with integrity the tasks on our list,

exploited and expendable. White men will not work that list.
Inert natives will nurture indifferent indolent sloth,
apathetic and lethargic. Harsh, hard and heavy work is
handed home to the culprits who cannot complain, who are here
seeking asylum from paupered privation, prisoners on
Manhattan. They wear many faces, but all nerves flash forth the

flinching flickers of fear from exposure, and this weakness the
bosses extort. What happened to the pioneer spirit? List
mundane jobs and we fine Uptown Women sag, slackened by sloth.
Machines wash the dishes, the clothes and the floors and the food is
pre-cooked, pre-packed, prepared without further effort from us. Here
is someone to iron and clean, to paint nails and primp hair and on

special occasions to cater for guests. Someone to take on
responsibility, bring up our young. Someone to walk the
dog. Someone to seek out the sales on the slick Saks shopping list
whilst we sluggishly shirk employment in our stupor of sloth,
lazing in inactivity, discontent. And the day is
determined by *TV Guide*, a mind void of exertion. Here

all feeling falls fallow, values bleach void, meaning melts, and here
the dancing Devil delves as money melds morality on
the slippery slopes of sin. Idle eyes seek diversions, the
glint of gossip grows like gangrene, making reality list
and sway in the dark and erotic imagination. Sloth
permits tittered tales to take on new dimensions and this is

dangerous. Shadows grow. Whispers echo and nastiness is
spread like rancid butter. Whatever small secret shimmers here
is magnified, mangled by boredom's tainted tardy thoughts, on
the rusted shelves of truth. We are so busy dealing with the
business of others, we neglect our own. We have a hate list
spawned by xenophobia; cannot recognize that this sloth

we cultivate permits foreigners to function freely here.
He oils the machine. He nurtures the lax void for in it is
his salvation. His family thrives, prospers and grows. On our sloth.

THE SIXTH SIN:
My big broad beam waddles down Broadway. Swathes of flab swaying, I
waddle on citrus peel legs in soggy skin, seeking to find
fast food consumables to curb cruel craving. Gluttony
peers past pig pop eyes. I voraciously stalk the delis there
panting for pastry and creaming for cake, intemperate as
a hog. I greedily gorge and gobble my fill, planning well

in advance the next mega meal. But once I was shaped as well
as the models who flash from the billboards and magazines. I
gave in to excess, found fulfillment in feasting, frowned to find
loneliness a gross woman caught, encased in greased gluttony.
With chewing came consolation; a full mouth could smile back. There
the beauty, mummified by mastication, was ensnared as

the beaver, by bingeing on buns. Attitudes changed as quick as
my clothing, men were repulsed and woman amused for how well
they shone in my shadows. Some wide nights, when shocked by mirror, I
sought solace in corner bars and woke one dark morning to find
that swigs would swill the day away, gulps of giggling gluttony.
On the outer frame my body bulges and sags. Inside there

sticky spheres grow. Cholesterol clogs the blood flow, is wedged there
like globs of gum, saturated fat. My liver lies leeched as
a sated slug, furry and fused, unable to function well.
Atheroma attacks the arteries. My heart sleeps a beat. I
stuff full the skin from the inside, frantically hoping to find
cessation of yearning, filling of void, end to gluttony.

There is no thinning back, Jell-O junkie, for the gluttony
is integral and the damage spawns a cankered mushroom there,
a gray fuzzy fungus. My own enemy, willpower as
fragile as a hymen, I still deny my options as well
as desire. Tramping the treadmill, tight trapped in the circle I
transcend love with the gourmet grub, revered like a treasured find

wormed deep in my core. Look beyond this cover and you will find
in the honeycombs of self-hate, essence marred by gluttony.
The lost little girl cries softly, hungry for happiness there,
hides her shame, is unwilling to battle with the demons as
they rise in a wave of want, yawning hollow from the hell well.
This is my purgatory and I suffer it every day. I

burn in fat and toil with your rejection, for this gluttony
is master. I know now there are as many cruel comments as
there are kinds of monster. And there is death by chocolate as well.

THE SEVENTH SIN:
Wanting the worn womb from whence he emerged, Oedipus stares and
stabs in his blindness, erases his father from view and the
raw guilt burns white in the black. Lust ladder rises to final
scenario. Penile umbilical knots madness to sin.
The unseen male malady, passed down through mythology, is
the universal cut. Moon man is doomed by his lechery.

Girlish games curdle sour like breast milk. Teenage lechery
hangs hard in her hips, a ripening rat in her daydreams and
future, gnawing and quickening. The youngster gives birth to the
baby, duped by fantasy and silver smooth words; a final
betrayal. Seduced and submerged in a plethora of sin,
drum taut and bursting, she cries and realizes this is what is.

Twin standards entwine through society; the division is
marked by tattling tongues who lustily lap up lechery
wounding the women with ruined reputations, slut soiled and
shoddy, whilst the males are encouraged in fornication; the
wanderer grins, is conquest crowned, but there is yet a final
rub: that boring virginity excuses venereal sin.

Damned by duty he says *I do* to sink within the skin sin.
Snared and shackled by church-clinked chains, mistakenly dreams he is
redeemed from Hell and dignifies his lewd, loin-filled lechery,
crucified on the cross of convention. His weak will wanes and
is welded to a woman without love. Sentence begins. The
future blinks blackly. These vows shall dissolve; will not be final.

Scented in stockings, she struts across Times Square for a final
trick. Cheapened by use, tacky and tarty, she is paid for sin
in the alleys and car seats, the pride of her pimp; and she is
only thirteen. Sucked from suburbs, lured by night lights - lechery
lanterns which glitter in greed - and the white snow which powders and
blinkers her brain, she is buried from reality and the

pain. Lust and pleasure, in exquisite tightness, squirt deep in the
muscles of man. Rapture runs rampant and explodes in final
feelings which permeate fear and succumb to seductive sin.
Narcissus clings to himself in the darkness but his joy is
blighted by blackened spots and the legacy of lechery
which will penetrate a population, bringing loathing and

death. A snake has entered the garden again and in final
victory it will spit on the pure souls, saturate with sin,
blight blood, making all of us writhe and fade in our lechery.

INKA PUBLICATIONS

POETRY SHOWCASE COMPETITION, 1996

INKA PUBLICATIONS PROUDLY PRESENTS THE WINNERS OF THE 1996

SHOWCASE POETRY COMPETITION

1ST PLACE - Ruth Zimmerman, *Dirge*
2ND PLACE - Alice Johansen, *Winter Trees*
3RD PLACE - Ruth Zimmerman, *Internal Combat*
4TH PLACE - Pietro DiLegge, *Two Shots*
5TH PLACE - Robin Sidwa, *The Bloated Blues*
6TH PLACE - Susan Marie Summers, *Healing*
7TH PLACE - Shea, *A Love, Unknown*
8TH PLACE - Jane M. Long, *Biorhythms*
9TH PLACE - Wayne R. Landry, *Ducks on Fruitcake...*
10TH PLACE - Melanie M. Averso, *Falling*

Judged by Susan Sanabria, Guest Editor

Dirge

by Ruth Zimmerman

As I walk the corridor
it is not sorrow I feel
but the sting

of the nurse's question
as she brings me a child
another woman bore.

I stand in robe and slippers
where I promised myself
I would not stand

looking into the nursery
at bed after bed
of the newest crop

trying to read names
and weights
trying to guess which

might best represent
the stringbean-like form
I baptized last night

and remembering
how more than anything
I felt relief

there would not be
a sixth child
in seven years.

Behind the glass
they wriggle and stretch
yawn and flail

crunch up purpling faces
in a cacophonous
song of distress

as I press my head
to the cold pane
uterus contracting
in emptiness.

Winter Trees

by Alice Johansen

Bare bones
imploring heaven.
The strain
of movement
creates
snapping, cracking,
splintering.

Softness
but a memory.
Rounded edges,
fluttering whispers,
long removed.

Like wooden nets
cast towards the clouds,
branches reach
up and up
to gather
rays of sun

and hold them captive
in dark,
cold,
brittleness.

Metamorphosing.

Internal Combat

by Ruth Zimmerman

it was the first time
I saw my mother cry
but not the last
during those solemn years
when a two-star banner
hung in the dining room window

from my hiding place
behind the secretary
I watched her rocking
reading the V-mail
and shook at her exploding words
alive injured hepatitis
O my God she said
and dropped to her knees praying
for her first born my brother

she was unaware of her youngest
her only daughter
crouching in the corner
blaming myself in childish confusion
sure it was something I had said
or hadn't said
sure it was something I had done
or hadn't done
sure of nothing
but the importance of sons

Two Shots

by Pietro DiLegge

Two shots
rang out

and a
country grieved

and a
world grieved

and we
each grieved

for a
life expired...

Two shots
rang out

and their
echo still

sounds through
the canyons

of time
affecting history

for eternity...

The Bloated Blues

by Robin A. Sidwa

Absorbent, marine invertebrate
in a brick-like frame work.
Dry, but most times not.

Porous, permeable personality
sits sodden in all our homes.
What a moist, parasitic swab
dampened by our clumsy moves.

Finally, its soggy body
leaks from saturation.
Poor perverse little sponge.

Healing

by Susan Marie Summers

I strain my eyes into the darkness of despair
I know something is there, I can sense it
A solitary stark white light strikes in the corner
Through the haze of my desolation I stare in disbelief

It lies there in a huddled mass, wrapped in defeat
The scent of hopelessness permeates the surrounding air
A closer scrutiny reveals the abuse unerased by time
Anguish suffered through the multiple indignities
Bruising perpetrated by constant direct assaults of pain

Blood trickling in uneven splotches of grief
Of unrequited love that has traveled through
The wrung out shadow of a soul unfulfilled
Endlessly clinging to hope, praying for the future

I approach this wounded mass of pain with caution
I hesitantly reach out my hand in a gesture of support
I stroke with soothing reassurance while cradling with love
I gently wipe away the pain, the blood, the tears

With time I sense the resurgent flow of strength
The compassion and caring gently recreated
The gates open up cautiously once again in trust and faith
With a steady slowness the healing travels its weary course
And my bruised and battered heart is ready for yet another battle

A Love, Unknown

by Shea

So close, so close,
yet really,
far apart.
My lips conceal,
what's in
my heart.
We barely
touch,
so much
within.
To be,
with you,
my private
sin.
I'm most
aware,
your voice
reveals,
from you,
yourself,
what you'd
conceal.

Biorhythms

by Jane M. Long

Sometimes
when I lie with you,
my head against your chest,
I listen to your heartbeat
and fear the time
when I will no longer hear it.
Of course,
it is inevitable
that one day,
one of us
will sleep alone.
For now,
I pull closer
and listen for
blood coursing through veins,
cells dividing,
dreams dancing on a web of neurons.
Daily,
we merge and part,
dive deep and surface,
memorizing our comings and goings,
and hedging our bets
on heaven.

Ducks On Fruitcake Rule The World

by Wayne R. Landry

If you could see me for what I really am,
What would you see before you?
Of all possibilities, certainly not Superman,
But someone similar too.

Contradictions of farces & truths
Testing liking & patience.
While the world around us still moves,
Not adding any distance.

Confessions shrouded in sheets of hot air -
Nothing is as obvious as this.
Be not discouraged - Love you can't wear,
But you can carry a kiss!

Falling

by Melanie M. Averso

Falling, falling fast.
Heart pounding, arms flailing
Trying to defy gravity
Gravity always wins.
Falling out of bed.
Falling with a crash.

Falling, falling fast.
Head pounding, face burning
Trying to avoid truth
Truth always wins.
Falling from grace.
Falling into sin.

Falling, falling fast.
Heart pounding, spirit bounding
Trying to deny love
Love always wins.
Falling into love.
Falling hard.

To order additional copies of **Show and Tell**, complete the information below.

Ship to: (please print)

Name ______________________________

Address ______________________________

City, State, Zip ______________________________

Day phone ______________________________

_____ copies of ***Show and Tell*** @ $8.50 each $ _______

Postage and handling @ $1.50 per book $ _______

New Jersey residents add 6% tax $ _______

Total amount enclosed $ _______

Make checks payable to ***Inka Publications, NJ.***

Send to: Inka Publications, NJ.
P.O. Box 53, Madison, NJ 07940-0053

- -

To order limited copies of **Collected Experience**, complete the information below.

Ship to: (please print)

Name ______________________________

Address ______________________________

City, State, Zip ______________________________

Day phone ______________________________

_____ copies of ***Collected Experience*** @ $8.50 each $ _______

Postage and handling @ $1.50 per book $ _______

New Jersey residents add 6% tax $ _______

Total amount enclosed $ _______

Make checks payable to ***Inka Publications, NJ.***

Send to: Inka Publications, NJ.
P.O. Box 53, Madison, NJ 07940-0053

